Z
is for
Zombie

an opuscule by
JT ARANT

Z is for ZOMBIE

an opuscule by

JT Arant

The author can be contacted at:
wordmechanics@gmail.com

This novella is a works of fiction. Any resemblance to actual events or locales or persons, living or dead, is purely coincidental.

ISBN: 9781692040277

To Winston,

Have a nice summer,

hope to see you again soon

A message from the author:

This is, obviously, a parody zombie novel. What may be less obvious is that it was inspired by a TV show called New Girl. So, I suppose, in away, it's Fan Fiction. One of the characters, Nick Miller, is an aspiring novelist, and after many many false starts, he finally completes a novel about zombies. The first few sentences of which were read out loud for the audience by another character, Winston Bishop. Upon hearing those first few lines, it became apparent to me that it was a story that deserved, nay *needed*, to be told in real life. For my parody, I kept those first few lines then let the story follow its own path. I hope I've captured the absurdity and flow that inspired it. Thanks New Girl.

Z is for ZOMBIE

No one in the sleepy mountain town of Rythm City knew what the meteor meant, but the one thing Mike Jr did have was a whole lot of rhytms.

"Whoa! What bit me in the face?" Mike Jr said to his dad, Mike Sr, who sucks. Mike Sr sucks a whole bunch, much more than his neighbor, Rollo.

Zombie Zoo, Zombie Zoo. Zombie Zoo, Zombie Zoo. Who let them zombies out? That damn Zombie Zoo.

Uh oh, watch your back, Laura.

Z	Y	P	O	N	I	D	R	J
U	Q	L	J	X	W	Z	I	C
E	I	G	L	A	F	O	O	S
V	H	P	F	N	N	I	E	B
O	M	W	C	E	G	O	N	T
M	O	H	T	M	S	R	P	A

The meteor lit the sky up like a flashlight. A really good one, like the kind the FBI use. It raced across the sky, leaving a trail of fire behind it and a promise of destruction in front. The good people of Ryhthm City stopped what they were doing and watched. They went out on their balconies, some went up to the roof, some just watched from a window, too lazy to go outside, but they all watched. Every last one of them. Some thought it was a shooting star, some thought it was a show, some new kind of fireworks display. Seatown was only a few miles away on the other side of China Woods and they were so smug, always showing off that they were bigger and richer than Rythm City. But they didn't have Rythm City's ryhthm. No one did.

The meteor didn't care about Rhythm City's rhymths though, it had places to be, it had places to go. As it went out of sight, everybody went back into their homes, back to their dinners and TVs and warm beds. It didn't just disappear though, it was in fact headed somewhere. It was headed to the zoo.

Rythm City Zoo is a good zoo, better than most. Almost like being in the actual wild, except with fences and conveniently spaced food and drink kiosks.

Bam! Smoke, fire, the whole bit. The meteor crash landed in the Gorilla Sanctuary. The great apes went, well, apes. They freaked out and ran for cover, some hiding behind rocks, some heading up into the trees. Only one ape, Gorilla Greg, was brave enough to investigate the smoldering rock that had invaded his home. In the distance, lions roared, birds screeched, hyenas laughed. The old zebra next to the gorillas whinnied, but Gorilla Greg kept silent. The curious cat had his tongue. He moved toward the meteor on all fours, his body swaying back and forth, ready for anything. Ready for everything. But not ready for this.

The meteor wasn't a rock at all, instead it was a disc, black and smooth and about the size of a manhole cover. A little bigger. But not much bigger. Gorilla Greg moved in closer, wanting to touch it but knowing better. The air around it was hot, real hot,

hot like a freshly made burrito, but the air closest to the disc was cool, cold even. Gorilla Greg reached out. As he did so, a black oily substance began seeping through the smooth black surface of the vaguely manhole cover sized disc. Each drop of the liquid swirled around the surface, confused and searching, before finally converging together at the point closest to Gorilla Greg's outstretched finger. The primate's eyes reflected his innocence and lack of understanding. He wasn't afraid because he had no idea of the danger that awaited him.

The oil took on a more defined shape, a spiraling cone shape, moving ever closer to Gorilla Greg's fingertip. Then suddenly, it jumped. It wrapped itself around his finger, squeezing and hurting Gorilla Greg's hand. Ouch. The mighty ape let loose a howl in the night, loud and filled with fear. The old zebra in the next enclosure reacted badly; it started spinning around, chasing its tail, working itself into a panic, then jumped clear over the six-foot high fence and bolted as far and as fast as it could go. The oily substance, meanwhile, kept moving its way up Gorilla

Greg's arm, winding its way toward his elbow, toward his shoulder, toward his neck. It reached up like a hand past the gorilla's chin, over its mouth and nose, grasping for the ape's big brown eyes, which were wide and dilated. The liquid slipped in through the gaps, sliding in between the cornea and the eyelids, oozing its way behind the eye and, eventually, inside it. Gorilla Greg's beautiful brown eyes turned black, black like black, and he let out another howl. This one was different, though. This one was angry. This one was dangerous.

* * *

"Bugs," Mike Sr explained. "I hate 'em. They ruin nature, they do."

Mike Jr put his hand up to his face where the bug bit him and felt a warm trickle of blood. He wiped it away and then held his stained fingers in front of his eyes, close enough to get a good look. It was blood alright. He considered the significance of it, the thin red liquid that pumps through his body, giving him life, and thought to himself, 'Jeez my dad sucks.'

Mike Jr wished his dad didn't suck so much. But he did. He sucked a whole bunch.

In actual fact, Mike Jr had something to tell his dad, something big, but he was finding it hard to find the right words. Rhthm he had, in abundance, but words were harder. A word misspoken is a monster unleashed. You wish you could take it back but you can't because once it's out there it takes on a life of its own. It carries weight and, worse, it carries consequences. The bad kind. Better to keep the words inside, safely contained where they can't hurt anyone except yourself.

"What do you think that was?" Mike Jr asked, referring to the meteor that had just streaked past overhead.

"Just Seatown showing off again," Mike Sr explained.

Mike Jr shrugged, he didn't really care. He really needed to say what he needed to say. "Hey, dad," he began.

"What?"

"So, you know how I'm studying law at the university, right?"

"I heard something about it."

Mike Sr was a sarcastic bastard.

"Well," hem, haw, "I dropped out."

Mike Sr didn't say anything, he just stared, glared, at his son.

"The thing is, see," Mike Jr began, feeling compelled to explain, "I've just got way too much rhthym to be a lawyer. My passion, my true calling, is to be a DJ. Maybe work as a bartender for a while because, you know, it's cool."

Mike Sr still said nothing, just looked at his son, disappointment dripping from his eyes. Eventually, it got to be too much for Mike Jr so he said, "Dad, please, say something." Mike Sr's answer was simply to get up and walk inside.

Mike Jr stayed out in the backyard. He was hoping to find and maybe take back a few of those misspoken words, so he could put them back in their box, but he couldn't. They were monsters now, they didn't belong to him anymore. Now it was up to the villagers to deal with them, to form an angry mob and trap them and burn them and other stuff like that.

Rollo, their neighbor just happened to be standing nearby, on the other side of the fence, and heard Mike Jr mumbling to himself.

"What's going on, Mike Jr?" he asked.

Mike Jr liked Rollo, he was a good neighbor. So Mike Jr explained his frustration. "I have a gift," he explained. "I've got so much rhthym. I just feel like I have to share it with the whole world, you know?"

"I do know," Rollo answered. "I've known you your whole life and I have always admired your rythme. But I also understand your dad's position."

"How can you say that!?"

"He just wants what's best for you, Mike Jr. Maybe you can't see that, because you're too close to the situation. You're too angry. Maybe you need to get away from here, go somewhere and think about your options."

Mike Jr knew Rollo was right. Rollo was always right. What a great guy. Not at all like Mike Sr, who sucked.

"In fact," Rollo added, "Maybe what you should do is talk to someone, a friend. A good friend. Someone who matters. You got anyone like that in your life, Mike Jr?"

"I do," Mike Jr answered. "I do."

That person was Carol.

* * *

The zebra pranced pretty down a poorly lit street. It didn't care that no one saw it, recognition is for those who need to be the center of attention. Zebras don't need that. All that zebra needed was to dance.

* * *

Mike Jr went to the place in China Woods where he and Carol first met. They were both sixteen at the time and a lot had changed since then, but it was still their spot. He paced back and forth, trying to grind down the anger and frustration he felt. How could Mike Sr not appreciate the power and significance of Mike Jr's rythms? He had so much of it.

He was still pacing back and forth when Carol showed up. Carol was pretty. Carol was real pretty. She was pretty and smart and rich, real rich. But that isn't why he loved her. No, Mike Jr loved her because she was pure and honest, because she was fair and decent. And because she was pretty, real pretty.

Carol raced over to Mike Jr, eager to hug him, eager to kiss him, on the lips, like lovers who do it. Mike Jr though wasn't in the mood. He was too damned angry. "Besides," he said, "William will be here in a minute."

"William?" Carol pouted. "Why do you like that

guy so much? It's kind of gay."

"I've known him my entire life," Mike Jr explained. "We were born on the same day, at the same hospital. His family lived across the street from mine. He's like my brother."

"Do you ever call him that?" she asked. "My brotha. Or would that be weird because he's black?"

Mike Jr loved Carol but her attitude toward William had always been a problem for him. Maybe it was because William was the only black person she knew? Everything else she knew about African American culture was the result of hours upon hours of sitting in front of the TV watching music videos and that show, 'In Living Color'. The one with the angry clown, what was his name?

Before Mike Jr could explain that William's skin color didn't matter, William arrived. He was wearing baggy pants, a skin tight T-shirt that drew attention to his muscular upper torso, and a baseball cap tilted to one side. He believed that he could mock the stereotypes by embracing them, he called it 'being ironic'. Ironically, most people didn't get that and so pretty much everyone thought he was just some guy trying to be a rapper. That's what they all look like, right? No one knew that in real life he was an accountant. Certified.

"I got your message, man. What's up?"

Mike Jr told them both about dropping out of school, his plan to be a DJ and the fight he'd had with Mike Sr.

"Your dad sucks," William said.

Carol agreed, then added that she thought Mike Jr would make a great DJ. "You've got so much rhythem. It's like you were born to do it."

Mike Jr said thanks. Rollo had been right, talking to his friends had made Mike Jr feel better. He was about to suggest that they go to their favorite diner, The Purple Cantaloupe, to grab a bite when they heard a sound coming from deep inside the forest, a sound born from the darkness of the trees. A sound like nothing any of them had ever heard before.

"What was that?" William asked. No one had an answer so, bravely, he said, "Stay here" and ventured into the darkness to investigate.

Carol looked at Mike Jr, flashed her big blue eyes and said, "So, you know in horror movies when the girl's like, 'Oh my God! There's something in the basement, let me just run down there in my underwear and see what's going on, in the dark.' And you're like, 'What is your problem!? Call the police!' And she's like, 'OK!' but it's too late because she's already getting murdered. Well, this feels a bit like that."

Mike Jr and Carol both laughed, because it was like that. Just like that. Hahaha.

Their laughter stopped though, when they heard a new sound. The sound of William screaming. Then there was a ripping sound and after the ripping sound there was nothing. Nothing until they heard, and saw, William's head flying through the air. It sailed just over their heads and they could see the crushed vertebrae and severed spine and the shredded tubing that used to be his neck. The head hit a nearby tree, thwapp!, thunk!, blood and mucus and ripped tendons and torn flesh was plastered against the bark. It was disgusting. But it was also kind of cool.

Carol screamed.

Mike Jr looked at her, she was looking over his shoulder and there was terror in her eyes, her big blue eyes. He looked back and saw Gorilla Greg emerging from the forest.

Gorilla Greg looked different than he remembered. He was bigger now, and more wild. His hair was matted and there were chunks of skin ripped off his chest and arms, showing the pink muscles underneath. His hands were bloody and his black eyes were red with anger. It was clear that Gorilla Greg wanted to kill them, though neither knew why, they had never been anything but nice to the animals at the zoo. Nevertheless, Mike Jr knew he needed to step up. He needed to embrace the Hemingway inside him, the Hemingway inside every man, and fight the gorilla.

Under normal circumstances, there's no way a man could defeat a gorilla in a fistfight, especially a gorilla that had been turned into a zombiefied monster version of its former self, but these weren't normal times, and Mike Jr wasn't a normal guy. He was overflowing with rythm. It was more of a dance than a fight, Mike Jr sliding this way then that, ducking under Gorilla Greg's heavy arms as they swung furiously, clumsily. Mike Jr jabbed when the opportunity presented itself but mostly he was just dancing. Eventually, faster than one might imagine in fact, Mike Jr saw his opening; he dove and rolled to his left, grabbing a heavy limb about the size of a baseball bat, and swung up. The thick branch connected with Gorilla Greg's chin, sending him backwards in a slow-motion cascade. The great ape crashed against a nearby tree and collapsed into a beaten heap.

Never underestimate the power of rythm, Mike Jr thought to himself.

Carol was still screaming. "What was that?" Mike Jr asked out loud, though to be honest he wasn't talking to anyone in particular. He looked at the decapitated head of his oldest friend and fought back a tear. It should have been me that went into the woods, he thought. He told Carol to calm down.

"It's over now," he said. "We're safe."

But no one is ever really safe though, are they? And that was true for Mike Jr as well, because even though he had easily defeated the gorilla in a fistfight, he had let his guard down and a zombiefied squirrel bit him on the ankle. It hurt like hell, but it was just a squirrel, so Mike Jr grabbed it and threw it hard against the same tree William's head had crashed against a few minutes earlier. Another thwapp!, another thunk!, more blood and guts.

Only it wasn't just a squirrel, it was a zombie squirrel. And it's not the size of a zombie squirrel that matters, it's the sharpness of its teeth. And the fact that it's a zombie. And that particular squirrel was both a zombie and it had sharp teeth.

Mike Jr looked down at his bloody ankle, felt his foot, then his entire leg go numb, and he collapsed to the ground. Now it was Carol's turn to step up. And she did so with aplomb. She helped Mike Jr to his feet and guided him over to her car. She put him in the back seat then set off for the hospital.

Unfortunately, she needed gas. Her father had warned her against letting the needle get too low but she never listened. So she was forced to stop at the first gas station she came across. It was called 'Stop And Go'. And that's exactly what she wanted to do. There weren't any other cars around but there was a light on and she knew it was still open. She told Mike Jr to hold on, then got out and filled her 1978 BMW 733i with unleaded gasoline.

She went inside to pay and the cashier, Spencer, said, "Weird night, ain't it?"

"What do you mean?" Carol asked, trying not to sound freaked out.

"They're saying a lot of weird stuff is happening."

"Who is they?"

"The radio. They say there was an accident at the zoo, some of the animals are sick, others have escaped, and they say they are dangerous. They say the police are rounding up anyone and everyone who has come in contact with them. It all sounds very weird to me."

"Weird indeed."

"I think if I see one of those animals, I won't tell anyone because I don't know what the cops are doing rounding these people up. You'd think they should go to the hospital, but apparently that ain't the case. Anyway, have a nice night."

"Yeah, you too."

Carol went back to the car and found Mike Jr sweating profusely. His skin was starting to turn gray and he couldn't respond to her questions. All he could do was moan. I need to get to the hospital quick, she thought to herself. Then she remembered Spencer's warning.

"I will take you to my home instead," she said. "I'm sure you'll be fine."

When Carol arrived at her home, her parent's home to be precise, she scanned the windows for lights to see who was there. Her parent's room was dark but the living room light was on, so she took Mike Jr around the back and down into the basement. Her parents never went down there, it's possible they didn't even know it existed. She had to sneak him in because, one, she didn't want her parents to call the hospital until she knew what was happening with all the other people who had been rounded up. And even though she hadn't actually heard of anyone being rounded up by the police she believed Spencer when he told her that it was happening. Why would he lie? He seemed like such a nice guy, and he had great hair. But there was another reason as well and that second reason was that her parents, her father in particular, didn't like Mike Jr very much. He thought Mike Jr wasn't good enough for his daughter. He didn't know how much rhthym Mike Jr possessed.

She got him into the basement, put him on the old sofa, covered him with a blanket, then raced upstairs to get some medical supplies. "What do you need to stop a zombie transformation?" she wondered out loud. She grabbed bandages and aspirin from the bathroom, then went to the kitchen to get some water. She grabbed three bottles of water, cradling them in her arms like a sick porcupine, when her brother, Jimmy, surprised her.

"What's going on, sis? Thirsty?"

Carol panicked. "No, yes, it's not for me."

"Who is it for?"

"It's for me," she lied. "Why are you asking so many questions?"

Jimmy looked her over suspiciously. He knew something was amiss.

"Everything is fine," she assured him. "No need to worry."

He knew he needed to worry, but Carol was a big

girl, not big as in big, but big as in mature, so instead of worrying he grabbed a slice of Irish bread and went back to his room to work on his novel.

Carol raced back down to the basement, arriving just in time to witness Mike Jr's transformation from human being to zombie. She was both afraid and disgusted and, yes, intrigued. She always had a thing for bad boys, and what could be worse than a zombie? Still, she knew he was dangerous and considered whether or not she should kill him. She grabbed a golf club, a driver with a heavy wooden head, and readied herself by aiming for his skull. There was something in his eyes though that stopped her. He wasn't human, not anymore, but he was still Mike Jr. And she still loved him.

* * *

And he still loved her. He had turned into a zombie, sure, but somehow he was still aware of himself and his surroundings. In fact, he didn't know he was a zombie at all. He wanted to touch her, to hold her in his arms and make her feel safe, to make himself feel safe, but his legs felt numb, like they were asleep, and when he moved toward her, it was more of a shuffle than a walk. He watched confused as Carol grabbed a golf club and lifted it up as if she were going to swing it at him. Mike Jr stopped when he realized that she was scared of him. But why would she be scared of him? It didn't make any sense, he couldn't understand it. He opened his mouth to tell her that everything was alright, that he was fine, but by that point words were nonexistent for him. In his mind he was saying, 'Carol, don't worry, it's me, Mike Jr, your boyfriend. Everything is going to be fine, just fine. Trust me.' But in reality what he said was, "Unngghhhh. Unnnghhhh."

He heard the gurgle that had replaced his words and began to realize that something was wrong. Something was very wrong. He noticed that, as he got closer to Carol, he could sense her blood. He could actually smell it, and it smelled good. In fact, she smelled better as a whole, like food, and he had this urge, a strong urge, to bite her. But he didn't. Because he loved her, and you don't bite people you love … unless they're into that sort of thing.

* * *

Meanwhile, back at Mike Sr's place:

Mike Sr and Rollo were in Mike Sr's backyard, drinking beer from the bottle and discussing Mike Jr's future. Rollo was super supportive of Mike Jr and reminded Mike Sr that his son had a lot of rythym. "Rhtym like that should be shared with the entire world," he said. "You know I'm right."

Mike Sr didn't know that at all and was about to explain why he disagreed when they heard a loud commotion coming from the street outside. They both got up and started walking toward the gate. They needn't have made the effort, because the commotion outside was coming to them. A zombie, in brown corduroy pants and a blue plaid shirt, crawled over the fence into Mike Sr's backyard. It scratched and pulled its way over the high wooden barrier. Mike Sr was angry. "Get outta here!" he shouted.

It was Rollo though who realized that their uninvited visitor wasn't just some punk kid. "I think we need to call the cops," he said. "I don't think this is just some punk kid."

The poorly dressed zombie approached the two men with drive and certainty. He was determined, which is normally a virtue but in this case Mike Sr found himself wishing this particular zombie was more of a slacker, like his son. "Just my luck," he said. "An entire generation of quitters, and I get the one zombie who has to follow through on what he starts."

He handed a deck chair to Rollo and said, "Here. You hold it off while I call 911."

Rollo took the chair and, holding it out like a lion trainer at the circus, held the zombie back while Mike Sr took out his cell phone and dialed the number. 9. 1. 1. The zombie was frustrated and let out a howl, deep and guttural. It both surprised and scared Mike Sr and caused him to drop his phone. Frustrated, he began stomping the ground with his feet like a spoiled child and accidentally stepped on the phone, crushing it under his boot. Turns out, Mike Sr is stupid too.

"Rollo, let me borrow your phone!"

Rollo explained, while still holding the zombie at bay, "I don't like the idea of being tethered to technology and so I don't have one."

"What!? Why!?"

"I could go into the details," he said calmly, "And perhaps at another time I will, but right this very instant I have other concerns."

"But that just doesn't make any sense," Mike Sr shouted, ignoring Rollo's other concerns. "Having the ability to communicate over great distances wirelessly is what separates us from the animals. In fact,...."

At that very moment, two more zombies come crawling over the fence.

"Tomorrow," Mike Sr said, "I am going to demand a refund from the guy who built this fence!"

"Today, though," Rollo interjected, "You are going to help me hold these bastards off. Grab a weapon and get over here!"

Mike Sr looked around but there wasn't anything he could use as a weapon against zombies. There was a garden hose but as far as he understood that only worked on the neighbor's dog. So, instead, he moved into a position behind Rollo. "Just long enough for me to think of something," he pleaded.

Rollo continued to hold off the zombies, all three of them by now. It was really quite impressive when you think about it, but it makes more sense when you remember that Rollo didn't suck as much as Mike Sr did. Mike Sr scanned the yard, looking for weapons and/or a means of escape. The door to the house was too far away and blocked by three zombies. The gate leading out to the street was closer, but there was no way they could make it, not with three surprisingly diligent zombies in the backyard. One, sure. Two, maybe. Three, no way.

So Mike Sr did the only thing he could think of,

he kicked Rollo in the knee, his bad knee, and as Rollo collapsed to the ground, Mike Sr gave him an extra hard push toward the pack of zombies. As the zombies swarmed, engulfing Rollo and smothering his screams, Mike Sr ran for the gate and managed to escape out into the street.

Well played, Mike Sr thought to himself. Well played.

Carol went to the grocery store to buy large quantities of meat. Specifically, she was buying large slabs of raw beef. She knew enough about zombie lore to understand that Mike Jr needed to eat, needed to feed, and she hoped raw meat would do the trick.

Just as she was perusing the barbecue sauce aisle, though, she heard someone call out her name. She recognized the voice and knew who it was before she ever even turned around: Tugg Masters.

Tugg was a man from Carol's past, an old boyfriend in fact. He was handsome and smart and, as far as Mike Jr was concerned, his mortal enemy.

Tugg went to the same university as Mike Jr. They were in the same class, in fact. But that's where the similarities ended. Tugg was the top student, whereas Mike Jr was struggling to survive. Tugg also had a lot of rythm and he was in a band, The Tugg Masters. Mike Jr's band, The Rythmic Groovers, was better, everyone said so, but Tugg had all the connections and that meant he got all the good gigs.

"It's great to see you," Tugg said, not trying to hide his excitement at all. "How are you these days? Seeing anyone?"

Carol hated that question. The fact is, she loved Mike Jr but she couldn't tell people that they were together because her parents would disapprove. They had, in fact, forbidden her from dating him, so Carol and Mike Jr were forced to keep their relationship a secret. Mike Jr had always hated that, but he understood. Carol, on the other hand, kind of liked it. It felt dangerous.

Carol considered Tugg's question. If she lied and told him that she wasn't seeing anyone, Tugg would be even more smug and, no doubt, ask her out and, honestly, she didn't want to have to deal with that. Especially not at that particular moment. Not when her zombie boyfriend was waiting for her in the basement. No, the easier thing would be to say yes. So she did.

"Really?" Tugg said, surprised and disappointed. "Who is this lucky guy? What's his name?"

Carol said the first thing that came to her mind: "Z."

"Z? What kind of name is that?"

"It's a nickname," she said, hoping that would be enough. It wasn't.

"You know my nickname is 'awesome'." He smiled, his hyper white teeth gleaming in the florescent lighting of the grocery store. "They call me that because I am the top student in the class and I have the best band at the university. Why do they call your man Z?"

Carol didn't answer, instead she went to the checkout counter and paid for her slabs of meat. Tugg followed her and asked again about the nickname. Just then, the song 'Gangnam Style' started playing through the store's loudspeakers and everyone groaned.

"I hate this song," Tugg said. "I hate this type of music, it's so fake."

"That's great," Carol said over her shoulder, not actually listening. All she wanted was to to get away from Tugg and back to Mike Jr.

Tugg wasn't willing to let her go quite so easily though and continued to follow her, this time out into the parking lot. Outside, away from prying eyes and the bright lights, he became a bit more aggressive. "Come on, Carol," he said. "You know you'd rather be with me than some loser named Z."

Carol got angry and told him to back off. But he didn't. He wouldn't. Instead, he moved closer to her and reminded her that she used to like being close to him.

"I was younger then. And stupid."

"I won't take no for an answer," Tugg insisted.

Carol didn't like where the conversation was heading and was about to scream when, out of nowhere, a wolf appeared. It was just standing there in the mostly empty parking lot, staring at Tugg. Tugg motioned for it to go away and shouted, "Shoo! Shoo!" The wolf responded by baring its massive, sharp teeth and snarling.

Tugg was terrified, but didn't want to show it so he looked at his watch and said, "Oh, look at the time. It's late, I should be getting back home. I am staying at my parents place, I'm just here for the week. If you want to come over and...." The wolf growled louder. Tugg said goodnight and left in a hurry.

Carol watched as Tugg's car, a Lamborghini, sped away, then she turned to the wolf, still standing in the parking lot, and said, "Thank you." The wolf, of course, didn't respond. It couldn't. It was a wolf.

Still, Carol felt an odd connection to it. She felt like she knew it somehow. She took a step toward it, but stopped when the wolf turned and disappeared back into the darkness.

M	X	J	R	Z	Y	Q	V	T
C	A	E	N	O	U	D	A	J
R	F	L	E	G	L	H	B	A
Y	P	Z	S	I	E	C	O	N
T	V	L	W	E	C	Y	M	O
L	S	H	R	A	D	T	P	Y
B	N	E	U	O	Z	U	O	I
D	Y	C	N	E	A	M	S	R
A	T	E	U	H	R	N	T	A

Mike Sr had been wandering the streets, not sure what to do. He thought about going to the police, but he knew he couldn't do that. How would he explain what he had done to Rollo. What he had done was really bad. So, instead, he went to Carol's place to ask if she knew where Mike Jr was.

"You can't be here," she told him, wondering if her parents were asleep upstairs and, if so, could they hear the conversation taking place on the front porch below?

"Just tell me where my son is," Mike Sr demanded.

Carol was torn. On the one hand, she should actually tell him. He was Mike Jr's father, after all, and he deserved to know what had happened to his son. On the other hand, though, he sucks. A lot.

"Just tell me," Mike Sr repeated.

"OK," she started, but before she could get any of the other words out, those tricky little bastards, a black van pulled up into the driveway and three masked men got out. They were wearing ski masks and looked tough. They ran over and grabbed Carol. Mike Sr could have tried to stop them. In fact, he probably would have succeeded, Mike Sr was a pretty big guy. But, instead, he stepped out of the way and, for the second time that night, he ran. Mike Sr is such a loser. Everybody knows it.

Carol struggled against the three masked men as they tried to put a black bag over her head. She kneed one right in the goolies and somehow managed to break free of them. She shouted out to Mike Sr as he ran down the highway toward Ryhytm City, hoping to convince him to come back and help her. He never stopped running though, so she was forced to run as well. Instead of following him down the highway toward Rhytm City, though, her instincts told her to go into the forest.

She ran and ran and ran and ran, but eventually the three masked men caught up to her. They surrounded her and tried to scare her with their cricket bats. Despite the urgency of the situation, Carol took a moment to note how odd that was ... cricket bats. No one played cricket in Rthyym City. It felt to her like a slightly pretentious choice of weapon and she said so: "Cricket bats? Really?"

The largest of the three masked men, the guy

she'd kicked in the jewels, took offense and shouted, "Shut up! Cricket is a beloved sport all around the world."

The voice was muffled under the mask and the pain that still burned in his groin, but she recognized it nonetheless.

"Tugg?"

The big guy sighed and dropped the bat. He pulled off the mask, revealing his square jaw and chiseled face.

"What are you doing?" she asked.

"Sorry, Carol," he said. "I just ... I don't know ... I wanted to scare you so I could save you. Don't you remember how we met? I rescued you from that guy who wanted to steal your purse? I thought if I did the same sort of thing...."

"What the hell, Tugg? This is unacceptable."

"So, are we not doing this?" one of the other men asked. "Because, technically, she could call the cops on us. I mean, what's that old guy going to do? He could be calling the cops right now for all we know."

"He's right," the other one said. "She knows who you are. She's a witness. You need to get rid of her."

"I know who you are too, Brad and Troy."

This upset the two men, who somehow thought she wouldn't recognize the voices of Tugg's two best friends after she had so efficiently recognized Tugg's voice. Troy, in particular, was worried. "I can't go to jail, I can't go to jail," he repeated over and over again, his voice cracking from the stress. He was on the verge of tears.

"Calm down, you're not goin...."

Tugg never got finish the sentence because the wolf finished it for him. It came out of nowhere and attacked Troy, who was closest to Carol, ripping out his vocal chord. He needn't have worried so much about going to jail. Blood spurted everywhere and Tugg, fearing for his life, reached into his pocket and pulled out a gun. That's right, a gun. After the incident in the parking lot, he had decided to bring the gun just in case. It was small and he'd had no intention of actually using it, but in the heat of the moment, well, he panicked.

Bang! The gun went off and the wolf squealed in pain. It collapsed to the ground, bits of Troy's neck still protruding from its mouth. Brad started crying, sobbing like a little child, and ran back toward the road, back toward the safety of Rthythm City. Tugg didn't know what to do so he followed, leaving Carol alone in the forest with the dying wolf.

Carol looked at Troy's bloody body and thought to herself, I never really liked that guy anyway. The wolf, though, the wolf she actually cared about. She knelt down beside it, ran her hand along its back, feeling the soft fur under her fingers. She also felt the warm sticky blood as it pooled out and onto the forest ground underneath them. She was sad and didn't know what to do. "Stay here," she said in a surprisingly calm voice. "I will go get my car and take you to a veterinary doctor. Just hold on."

"No," the wolf said.

* * *

Mike Jr was stuck in the basement. He was frustrated and becoming increasingly agitated. He was hungry. The raw meat was OK, it held the hunger at bay, but he wanted/needed something more.

He heard the commotion coming from the front porch and seeing that there was a small window, at ground level, he shuffled over to see what was happening. It broke his heart that he could only shuffle, there wasn't much rhthym to it.

From his vantage point, he was looking up, watching his father interrogate his girlfriend when the three masked men arrived. He shouted out a warning: "Mmmmaaaaannnggghhhh."

No one heard him though and he watched helplessly as his father ran away while Carol, the love of his life, was being accosted. He was embarrassed by Mike Sr's behavior but, more importantly, he needed to save Carol. He pounded at the window, trying to break it or perhaps simply trying to let the three masked men know he was there and that he would come for them. But, again, his perspective was different from reality. In his mind he was pounding away at the window, smashing his fists into it, on the verge of breaking it. In reality, though, all he could manage was a creepy scratching motion. Scratch. Scratch.

He watched helplessly as Carol struggled against the three masked men. But she wasn't as helpless as he, and when her right knee connected hard into the breadbasket of one of the assailants, Mike Jr felt a combination of pride and sympathy pain in his own rhthym basket. Ouch.

He watched as Carol broke free, called out to his father and then ran into the woods. He watched as the three masked men followed after her, one of them running a little bit slower than the others.

And he watched as Jimmy, Carol's brother, came running out after them, following them into the woods.

What he saw next was impossible.

* * *

The wolf, dying, transforms itself from a dying wolf into a dying human.

"Jimmy!"

Carol never saw that coming. No one did. It was a twist.

"Carol," Jimmy said, his voice raspy and failing. "I have something I need to tell you."

"What!?"

"I'm a wolf."

Carol didn't believe him. It was too weird. And unexpected.

"How?" she asked.

"Carol," Jimmy said, his voice raspy and failing. "I have something I need to tell you."

"What!?"

"You're a wolf too."

Carol collapsed to the ground and began crying. She didn't want to be a wolf.

"Carol," Jimmy said, his voice raspy and failing. "I have something I need to tell you."

"What!?"

"Mom and Dad ... they aren't our real Mom and Dad. We were adopted."

Carol cried some more. She didn't want to be adopted.

"Our real parents were Gypsies. They brought us here all the way from New Jersey."

Carol began to sob. She didn't want to be from New Jersey.

"Why are you still crying?" Jimmy asked. "Don't you get it? We are special. We have magical wolf powers."

Carol considered that and realized that, yes,

having magical wolf powers did not suck. Having magical wolf powers was, in fact, pretty awesome.

"Avenge me," Jimmy told his sister. "Find Tugg Masters and hurt him where it hurts."

"You mean...?"

"Yes."

Carol had qualms. She wasn't even sure what qualms were but she knew she had them. Tugg deserved to die, he had killed her brother. And he was a jerk. But, at the same time, it had been an accident, killing her brother, and, technically, he was just trying to defend himself against Jimmy who had turned into a wolf and was trying to kill him. It wasn't an entirely unforgivable thing.

"Avenge me," Jimmy repeated.

"I don't think I can," she said. "I'm not strong enough."

"You will be," Jimmy said, after coughing up some blood. "Just repeat this magical incantation that

Frank told me."

Carol agreed and knelt beside her brother again, leaning her head in close so she could hear the words. She repeated them:

"Zombie Zoo, Zombie Zoo.   Zombie Zoo, Zombie Zoo."

Suddenly, Carol felt an overwhelming sense of power. Her eyes started to glow, her teeth became sharper, and she knew then what she had to do.

Out on the highway to Ryhthm City, Mike Sr was running, trying to escape the three masked men. It was a slow run. There was a low red moon in the sky, and a thick fog everywhere else. The only sounds Mike Sr heard were his own, the clippity-clop of his feet against the hard road and a very heavy wheezing. He tried to keep running, but he couldn't do it anymore. He was too tired. He should have taken Mike Jr's advice and gone to the gym with him, but he didn't because he thought that was a stupid waste of money and time. Well, Mike Sr, who is stupid now?

Mike Sr stopped, looked forward, where he could just barely make out the bright lights of Rythym City blinking ryhtmically in the distance. He was almost home. He looked back, as well, just to be safe, and saw nothing. He put his hands on his knees and tried to catch his breath. But like those words earlier, it was gone and it wasn't coming back. He collapsed to the ground, lay back on the cold hard surface of the road and listened to the fog. It sounded pretty much like nothing, but that was OK. Mike Sr needed a little bit of nothing for a change.

The nothing didn't last long though because, soon, he heard something. It was quiet at first, a scratching sound. It lacked rhythhm. It was clumsy. It sounded like feet being dragged across asphalt. In the fog, though, he couldn't tell how far away it was. But he knew it was coming closer because it got louder and louder. It got real loud, in fact.

And then he saw them. Two zombies, emerging from the fog, moving toward him slowly but surely. Mike Sr sighed. He was sick and tired of all the running.

"Aaaarrrgghhh!" he screamed. "I just want to be home, watching basketball. The Rythym City Rthyms are playing Seatown on TV. Is that too much to ask for!?"

The zombies didn't answer. But they did shuffle their feet a little bit louder.

Mike Sr tried to stand up so he could start running in the opposite direction, back toward Carol's home, but his muscles hurt too much, his legs were like jelly, and he collapsed to the ground. Oh no, he thought.

The zombies shuffled closer, close enough for him to realize who they were. It was William and Rollo. And for a moment, Mike Sr was relieved. These were his friends, people who knew him. But then he remembered that he sucks and he could see in their big bloodshot eyes that they knew exactly who he was, and they also knew exactly what they were going to do to him.

Mike Sr's scream was loud and the fog carried it far far away into the night. All the way to Rythym City.

Carol rode the zebra (yes, THAT zebra) to Tugg's house. She knew he would be there, that he would be in the basement, because he had a pretty amazing mancave down there. He had beer, booze and a big TV. And lots of room to dance whenever the rhthym demanded it. All the stuff you need for an amazing mancave.

He also had a foosball table, but Carol wasn't impressed by that.

She kicked in the door with her new wolf power, and the door few off its hinges. It crashed against the wall, smashing his 40 inch flatscreen TV to bits. Tugg cried out, partly from fear but also partly from the horror of having his 40 inch flatscreen TV be smashed to bits, and fell to his knees.

"Please," he begged.

Carol, though, was in no mood for forgiveness.

She grabbed his cricket bat as she walked toward him. She felt the weight of it in her hand and whirled it around a bit. It felt good. It felt even better when she whacked Tugg on the head with it.

Pretentious maybe, but very effective.

* * *

When Tugg came to, he was tied to a chair. The room was dark, there was only one light, a hanging overhead light that shone brightly in his face. It was bright. So bright. He tested the strength of the ducktape that held his hands and feet to the chair. It was strong. So strong. He couldn't move an inch.

He didn't know where he was, but he knew the song playing in the background: Gangnam Style.

"So," he said, assuming Carol was hiding somewhere in the darkness. "You're trying to torture me with rythyms. Well, it's not going to work."

"Really?" she asked. "Why not?"

"Because I lied earlier, I actually like this song.

It's got lots of rthym, just like me. The joke's on you."

"Are you sure?" she said, stepping into the light. She was wearing something sexy; black and tight fitting. She walked around Tugg, circling him, letting him know that she was in charge and that he was merely prey. She leaned in close and whispered in his ear, her breath hot and sexy. "If you like the ryththm so much, why don't you dance?"

But, of course, he couldn't, and that was the real torture. Rythm torture.

"Let me go, Carol. You don't want to do this."

"Oh but I do," she corrected. "I really really do."

Tugg shook his head, he smiled. "Come on, Carol. It's me, Tugg. You know me, I'm a good guy."

"No you're not. You're really not. In fact, you suck. Almost as bad as Mike Sr."

"Carol!" Tugg shouted. "This isn't funny anymore! Let me go!"

"Nope."

"What do you think you're going to accomplish here, Carol? You don't have it in you to harm me."

"Maybe I didn't," she explained. "But that was before you killed my brother."

"What!? Jimmy!? I never killed Jimmy."

Carol got right up in his face and corrected him. "He was the wolf."

"The wolf? How is that possible?"

"We're both wolves," she explained, as she swayed to the ryththm of the song and did the little dance. "It's our special power, and it's pretty awesome."

It was pretty awesome, Tugg conceded. But how was he supposed to know that?

"I didn't know," said pleaded.

He wasn't wrong, which is why Carol had something else in mind.

She turned on the main light and Tugg realized that he was in her basement. He looked around nervously, looking for a way to escape. He was in the middle of the room, though, and there was nothing around him that could help. Except of course the pile of cow bones that littered the far corner of the room.

"What the hell have you been doing down here, Carol?"

"It's not what I've been doing that should concern you."

Then Tugg heard a noise. It was low and hollow, a moan, and he couldn't tell where it was coming from. Soon though scratching was added to the moaning and Tugg was able to determine that they were both coming from the closet.

"What is that?" he asked. "Who's in there?"

"That's Z."

"Z?"

Carol started walking over to the the closet.

"That loser?" Tugg said, smugly. "Is he supposed to be scary? Because, seriously, Carol, my name is Tugg. I'm not going to be intimidated by someone named Z. Get real."

"This is as real as it gets," Carol said. "And you should be intimidated. He's got a whole lot more rhythm than you."

Tugg didn't believe her, but the insult hurt him nonetheless.

"What does that even stand for anyway?" he asked, trying to throw the insult back in her face. "Z? Does it stand for Zack?"

Carol didn't answer.

"Then it must stand for Zitface. Or maybe it stands for Zero?"

He laughed at his clever little joke.

Carol put her hand on the doorknob and laughed as well. Then, as she turned it, she answered him:

"Z is for Zombie."

Z is for ZOMBIE

Other works by JT Arant

Playing Dice With The Universe

The Happy Damned

Rebel

The Long Of It and The Short Of It

The Warning Bell

Unspoken Truths

Once, a Collection of Poems

Made in the USA
Middletown, DE
28 December 2021

57198621R00038